Party Crashers

written and illustrated by Jonathan Roth

ALADDIN

New York London Toronto Sydney New Delhi

ALADDIN

An imprint of Simon & Schuster Children's Publishing Division
1230 Avenue of the Americas, New York, New York 10020
First Aladdin hardcover edition March 2018
Copyright © 2018 by Jonathan Roth
Also available in an Aladdin paperback edition.
For information about special discounts for bulk purchases, please contact
Simon & Schuster Special Sales at 1-866-506-1949 or business@simonandschuster.com.
The Simon & Schuster Speakers Bureau can bring authors to your live event. For
more information or to book an event contact the Simon & Schuster Speakers Bureau
at 1-866-248-3049 or visit our website at www.simonspeakers.com.
Book designed by Nina Simoneaux
The illustrations for this book were rendered digitally.
The text of this book was set in Adobe Caslon Pro.
Manufactured in the United States of America 0218 FFG
2 4 6 8 10 9 7 5 3 1
Library of Congress Cataloging-in-Publication Data
Names: Roth, Jonathan, author, illustrator. Title: Party crashers / written and
illustrated by Jonathan Roth. Description: First Aladdin paperback edition. |
New York : Aladdin, 2018. | Series: Beep and Bob ; 2 | Summary: Beep and his best
friend, Bob, are accused of stealing guests' jewelry during Lani's birthday voyage on
luxurious *Starship Titanic*, but things go downhill when *Titanic* plummets toward
Neptune. Includes facts about Neptune.
Identifiers: LCCN 2017018330 | ISBN 9781481488556 (pbk) |
ISBN 9781481488563 (hc) | ISBN 9781481488570 (eBook)
Subjects: | CYAC: Space ships—Fiction. | Birthdays—Fiction. | Parties—Fiction. |
Outer space—Fiction. | Human-alien encounters—Fiction. | Science fiction. |
BISAC: JUVENILE FICTION / Science Fiction. | JUVENILE FICTION /
Action & Adventure / General. | JUVENILE FICTION / Readers / Chapter Books.
Classification: LCC PZ7.1.R76 Par 2018 | DDC [Fic]—dc23
LC record available at https://lccn.loc.gov/2017018330

For Mom and Dad

★ CONTENTS ★

Party Crashers

★★★★★

SPLOG ENTRY #1:
Star Bores

Dear Kids of the Past,

Hi. My name's Bob and I live and go to school in space. That's right, space. Pretty sporky, huh? I'm the new kid this year at Astro Elementary, the only school in orbit around one of the outer planets. There's just one micro little problem: SPACE IS STUPENDOUSLY BORING!

I mean, sure, you can spend about two minutes

staring out giant picture windows at the infinite wonders of the universe. But then what? We're so far from Earth, the television reception is terrible. And the only channel that does come in well is—don't say I didn't warn you—*educational*.

Beep just said, "Beep like watch *Star Words*! Learn from robot ABCD-2!" Beep is a young alien who got separated from his 600 siblings when they were playing hide-and-seek in some asteroid field. Then he floated around space for a while, until he ended up here. Sad, huh?

You know what's even sadder? I was the one who found him knocking on our space station's air lock door and let him in. Now he thinks I'm his new mother! But since he also thinks *Star Words* is a good show (even though it's for three-year-olds), you can tell he's a little confused.

But I still like him.

"Beep like Bob-mother, too!"

Beep is pretty good at drawing, so I let him do all the pictures for these space logs (splogs, as we call them) before sending them back in time for you to read. Just don't hold me responsible if he only doodles his favorite *Star Words* alpha-bots.

Anyway, that's my life. Enjoy!

★★★★★

SPLOG ENTRY #2:
Party Invites from Heaven

kay, I know I just said space was pretty much the most boring thing ever, but that was *before* I had to sit through our class history reports. Each student had to choose a book about a historical event and report back to the class.

After listening to Zenith drone on about the first moon missions, and Blaster share every detail about World War P, I didn't think there was any history *left.* My brain was seconds from shutting down.

"Very good, children," Professor Zoome said when they were done. "Sadly, we don't have time for more today. We will resume on Monday with"—she checked her clipboard—"Bob."

Beep clapped. "Bob-mother, yay!"

Gulp. I wasn't even halfway through the book I'd picked out yet! I leaned toward Beep and whispered, "Luckily, she didn't say *which* Monday."

"And by Monday," she continued, "I mean the day after the day after tomorrow."

Beep clapped again. So much for a nice, quiet weekend staring out the window.

Lani grabbed my arm when I was halfway out the classroom door. Lani (short for Laniakea Super-cluster) is my best friend at school who *isn't* a confused alien. Not that I think about her a lot or anything, but "Lani" means "heaven" in Hawaiian. Of course, "Lani" can also mean "sky," depending on—

"Hey, Beep! Hi, Bob! I'm glad I caught you," she said. "Are you doing anything this weekend?"

My face grew hot. "Well . . . ," I began.

"Great!" She pulled out a couple of envelopes. "Because I'm inviting you both to my birthday party!"

Birthday party? I broke into a cold sweat. "There's not going to be a clown, is there?"

She shook her head. "No. Why?"

"My parents hired a clown for my birthday once, and I had to hide in a closet the whole time."

Lani smiled. "No clown, Bob. I promise."

"Whew. But, uh, what about

a magician? Because there was
this other incident—"

"No magician either."

"Swell. And no guy in
a purple dinosaur suit?"

"Bob, how many traumatic
birthdays have you had?"

I counted on both hands. "Pretty much all of
them."

"Well, this one's going to be different," she said.
"Just be sure to bring a bathing suit."

"You're having a pool party?"

"There's a pool in the water park."

I perked up. "Water park?"

"Actually, where we're going, there are three water
parks."

"*Three* water parks?"

"But if those aren't your style, there are also sixteen amusement parks."

"Sixteen amusement parks!"

"Though, if that's too tiring," she said, "I suppose you could stay in your room and surf the twelve million hypershow channels."

I began to drool. "Tw-tw-twelve million?"

"It's a lot, I know," Lani said. "But my parents insisted on having the party on some amazing new star cruiser that's taking a tour around Neptune. I hope you don't mind."

I shook my head. "We can handle it."

"I'm so glad!" Lani said. "We leave tomorrow and get back Sunday night."

Beep pulled on my sleeve. "When Bob-mother do big report?"

I pushed him away. "Silly Beep! He's always

joking." But when Lani was gone, I added, "Don't worry, Beep. I'm sure I can fit in my homework somewhere in between SIXTEEN AWESOME AMUSEMENT PARKS!"

I tore open the invitation. It read:

Lani is having a party!

On the maiden voyage of

the *STARSHIP TITANIC*!

Motto: The 100% Safest Ship in the Galaxy.

100% Guaranteed!

"Hmm, that name sounds familiar," I said, reaching into my backpack for the book I chose for my report (mainly because it was the only history book in graphic novel form I could find). It was about some ship that sailed on Earth a really long time ago (even for you kids of the past).

I read the title: *Titanic: A Night to Remember.*

"Look, Beep, the ship in my book has the same name as the one we're going to fly on for Lani's party."

"How book end?" Beep asked.

I shrugged. "I haven't gotten that far yet. Frankly, even history *comics* are kind of dull." I shoved the book back into my pack.

"What if end bad? *Starship* end bad too?"

"Don't be silly, Beep. It's the 'One Hundred Percent Safest Ship in the Galaxy. One Hundred Percent Guaranteed!' Even *I* won't be nervous about rocketing around space for a change."

Beep clapped. "Bob-mother no scared!"

"Yep! For the first time in my life, Beep, I think it's all going to end just fine."

★★★★★

SPLOG ENTRY #3:
All Present

We were supposed to be packed and ready for the voyage by noon Saturday, but I was so excited that I woke extra early: 11:49.

I unstrapped myself from my bed, floated out from the sheets, and called to the top bunk, "Wake up, Beep, we have to go!"

But his bed was empty. "Beep?" I spun to see him sitting at his desk.

"What are you doing?" I said. "Homework?"

"Beep watch *Star Words*!"

On screen, C-345 was teaching ABCD-2 the correct way to spell A-S-T-E-R-O-I-D. I gave Beep a once-over. "Have you been watching that all morning?" I asked. His eyes had that orange glaze that appears when he doesn't sleep for at least eleven hours.

"Plus night," Beep admitted.

I pushed the off button. "We're going on an overnight trip. We have to pack." I began shoving stuff in my backpack. "Bathing suit, check. Toothbrush, check. Pack of gum, check. Extra underwear, check. Extra pair of socks, check."

"Socks, yum!" Beep said, pointing to his tummy.

I sighed. "Make that *ten* extra pairs of socks." Soon my backpack was bulging. "So why does it feel like I'm forgetting something?"

"More sock?"

"No, something else." I scanned the room. "Well, I guess it can't be all that important."

Beep patted his pouch (when Beep eats something, it either goes into his eating tummy or his pouch tummy). "Beep have all need here."

"Then we're off!"

« * « ✪ » * »

Sadly we had to take the Astrobus (motto: 100% *Smell*iest Ship in the Galaxy) to get from school to the *Starship Titanic*.

Lani was waiting by the bus door. "There you are, Bob. I was worried you weren't going to make it on time. Everyone else is already here."

"Sorry. Just making sure I packed enough socks."

She studied my backpack and smiled. "Looks like there must be something more than just *socks* in there."

"No, pretty much just socks." I rolled my eyes. "Beep eats them by the dozen."

"Socks yum!" Beep said.

Lani winked. "Okay, Bob, *socks*. I'll take your word for it."

"What else would I have in here?" I asked as Beep and I floated aboard the bus.

Before she could answer, I froze. Lani's other friends were already seated . . . with big, fancy wrapped gifts on their laps!

"Oooh, pretty," Beep said, fawning over all the sparkly bows and ribbons.

I slouched into my seat and strapped myself in. "Uh, Beep," I whispered as the Astrobus took off. "You didn't happen to buy Lani a birthday present, did you?"

"What that?"

"Something you get someone to show how much you care about her."

"What Bob-mother get Lani?"

"Well, that's the problem," I admitted.

Beep gasped. "Bob-mother bad!"

"Hey, you didn't get her anything either."

Beep's eyes welled with tears. "Beep bad too!"

"No, Beep, shh, it's fine," I said. "You didn't know."

Beep nodded. "Sometimes good not know."

"Tell me about it," I agreed.

"Bob-mother not know lot of things."

"Well, I wouldn't say—"

"Bob-mother know *any*thing?"

"I know I have to find a good gift, Beep. And fast." I rummaged in my pack. "She told me once she likes gum."

Beep reached into his pouch. "Beep have pencil!"

"I doubt that's enough."

He broke it in half. "Two pencil?"

"Uh . . ."

He put it back. "Beep keep thinking."

I unwrapped a piece of gum and sank into my seat. "Bob-mother too."

But my thoughts were soon interrupted by a chorus of oohing and aahing. Beep pulled my sleeve. "We there!"

I straightened to look out the window. "Whoa," I said, shielding my eyes. "If that's the *Starship Titanic*, it's as bright as the sun."

"That *is* sun," Beep said, and spun me around to the window on the opposite side.

"Whoa!" I said, shielding my eyes even more. The massive star cruiser loomed before us like a floating city of lights. "Beep, have you ever seen such a sight?"

"Ooh! Aah!" Beep answered, but then I realized he was watching the video screen on the seat back in front of him. "ABCD-2 yay!"

I grabbed my backpack. "Beep, we're docking. And you're about to have your choice of twelve million *real* channels. Let's go!"

★★★★★

SPLOG ENTRY #4:
Gravity Falls

ne of the ship's stewards—another word for really fancy helpers—met us as we floated onto the deck of the *Starship Titanic*. "Watch your step," he said.

I winked. "Good one," I said to him, because there are no "steps" in space; the zero gravity thing takes care of that! We float *everywhere*.

Then I tripped over my feet and crashed into the floor.

"WHEEEE!" Beep said, doing the same.

"Need some help?" Lani asked. She gripped my hand and pulled me up.

"You didn't tell me they had gravity here," I said. Gravity is super expensive in space, so the ship had to be high-end.

"My parents say this ship has everything," Lani said.

"Yeah, like something for super rich people," I said. "I'm sure glad our tickets are free."

"Speaking of my parents, there they are!" Lani said. "Mom, Dad, over here!"

"Uh, the tickets *are* free, right?" I said.

Lani didn't answer me as her parents approached, trailing a line of stewards who carried their luggage.

Each steward gripped a suitcase in each hand and tucked a bag under each arm. I bet *they* weren't super happy about all this gravity, since it makes objects heavier!

"Laniakea, darling, how nice to see you," her mother said.

Lani gestured to the bunch of us. "Mom, Dad, these are my friends: Beep and Bob and Zenith and Flash and Andromeda and the rest."

Her parents shook our hands. "Pleased to meet you, Beep and Bob and Zenith and Flash and Andromeda and the rest."

Her father snapped his fingers, and a dozen more stewards appeared. "Please take our guests' belongings and escort them to their cabins."

Lani reddened. "It's okay. We don't mind carrying our own things."

But one steward had already taken my backpack, and another picked up Beep.

"Wait, he's not luggage!" I said.

"Is too!" Beep said, and whistled as the steward carried him along.

Lani walked next to me as the group followed the steward to our rooms. "Sorry about that. My parents are, well, used to having people do things for them."

"Cool!" I said.

"Sometimes," she said. "But just because we have help doesn't mean I think I'm better than anyone."

"So your parents have money?" I asked.

Zenith, on the other side of me, whispered, "Bob, you dolt. Lani's parents are the owners of Super-cluster Industries!"

"What's that?"

Zenith rolled her eyes. "Only one of the biggest companies in the solar system."

"Wow," I whispered, and then I started to put it all together. "Hey, Lani," I said, "did you know your parents are *rich*?"

She stared ahead. "Perhaps."

"I mean, *really* rich."

"Perhaps!"

The steward stopped and turned to me. "This is your room, sir."

"I'm a *sir*?" I said.

"Yes, sir."

Beep jumped out of his arms. "Beep sir too! Beep sir too!"

"Yes, sir."

The steward opened the door and led us inside.

"The room is equipped with the finest amenities in seven dimensions, but if you should need anything else, please push this red button and I will be back to assist."

Beep pushed the button.

"Yes, sir?" the steward said.

"Beep need hug."

"Yes, sir," the steward said, bending to put his arms around Beep.

"Now Beep need carry to bed."

"Certainly, sir."

"That's okay," I said. "Beep can walk."

Beep pointed across the wide room. "But bed far."

The steward handed Beep a remote control. "This will bring the bed to *you*, sir."

Beep pushed a button and the bed began to hover. Beep clapped and jumped on.

"Will that be all, sir?"

"Yes, thank you," I replied. Then I said good-bye to Lani and the others, who left to find their own rooms.

The second they were gone, Beep began to fly his bed in circles. "WHEEEE!"

"Could you stop that, Beep? I'm dizzy just watching you."

"Then no watch!" he said, switching to figure eights. He was pretty good with that thing.

"I'm going to unpack," I said, heading toward the dresser.

Just as I was stashing away the last of my socks, there was a knock at the door. It was Lani and the rest of the group. "Uh, hate to interrupt the fun, but want to go have some more fun?" she said. "We're heading to the rides!"

"Sure, let me catch Beep, and we'll meet you there."

"We'll be at the Super Nova Infinity Drop, Bob. See you soon!"

I waved at Beep. "Beep, c'mon. Get down so we can go." But he had found the video clicker, and suddenly a giant hyperscreen appeared in the room. "Oh, no, not *Star Words*."

Beep clicked to a shopping channel, where they were advertising precious stones. "That good birthday present for Lani-friend! Beep buy?"

"Not now, Beep."

"Now?"

I knew I had to buy Lani a gift, but it could wait. "Sheesh, Beep, we'll have plenty of time to buy her something later. Don't you want to go on some rides?"

Beep jumped off the bed, then pushed the red button. Within moments the steward appeared again.

"Yes, sir?"

"Beep want hug bye."

"Certainly, sir."

And then we were off.

★★★★

SPLOG ENTRY #5:
Ups and Downs

The amusement parks took up a massive section of the star cruiser's enormous domed deck. I studied a map inside the gate. "Right now we're at the baby park. But each park gets more fun until"—I zoomed in—"the Super Nova Infinity Drop!"

"Ooh," Beep said.

"Ooh is right. It says the ride is so fast it actually

warps through time. One ride only takes seconds, but seems like three hours."

"Aah!"

Truthfully, it sounded a little scary. "Of course, Beep, if there's *another* ride you want to go on first . . ."

Beep pointed and took off in a flash. "There!"

I ran to keep up. "But that's a *little* kid ride."

Beep didn't care. "Balloon Blast! Balloon Blast!" he said, reading the sign.

A bored-looking man in charge of the ride said, "Each of you sit on one of those chairs. Then I'll tie on just enough balloons so you can float."

"What's fun about this, Beep?" I asked. "We float all the time."

"Not with balloon!"

After we sat, the man entered the number 15 on

some machine called a Balloon-o-Matic, pushed a button, and fifteen floating balloons on strings suddenly appeared. He tied them to my seat and studied Beep. "You'll need about thirty."

"Beep want billion!"

"That would be enough to lift this entire ship!" the man said.

Beep clapped. "Yay!"

The man gave Beep an annoyed look. "You get thirty. And here's a needle; don't lose it. Next!"

Once the man let our chairs go, we began to float up, up, up, and . . .

"Beep, we're only about five feet off the ground," I said.

Beep glanced down. "Oooooh. Aaaaaah."

A girl who looked like she was four years old floated past me and stuck out her tongue. Off in the distance, the Super Nova Infinity Drop flashed like a beacon of *real* fun.

"This is lame, Beep. Let's get off." I waved at the man below. "Excuse me, but we're ready to get down."

"That's why I gave you a needle, kid!" he shouted back. "Just reach up and pop."

I tensed. "But . . . but I don't like popping balloons!"

The man shrugged. "Welcome to my world."

"Bob-mother scared of pop?" Beep said.

"Not *scared*," I said. "Just a weensy bit terrified. You see, it all began at one of my early birthday parties. The one with the, you know, *clown*."

★ 31 ★

"Beep not scared!" Beep said, reaching up to a balloon with his needle. I flinched at the sudden explosion. He lowered by a foot or two. "Now Bob-mother turn."

I lifted the sharp needle toward the closest balloon. An inch away. A half inch away. A half a half inch away. A half a half a half . . .

"Bob-mother take long time," Beep said.

"Don't rush me!" I said. "Okay, here goes." The needle pressed into the balloon. But nothing happened. I pushed a little harder. Still nothing.

"Uh, I think this needle might not be sharp enough," I called down to the man.

"Or maybe you're not strong enough!" he called back. The four-year-old floated past me and stuck out her tongue again.

"Here, Beep help," Beep said, grabbing my foot

and yanking until we were even again. He pointed his needle at one of my balloons.

"No, wait, Beep, I . . . AHHH!" I said at the sudden sound.

"One pop for Bob-mother!" Beep said. "One pop for Beep! One pop for Bob-mother! One pop for Beep!" And so on, for what felt like an endless descent. But finally, we made it.

I crawled off the seat, trembling, just as Lani and the others came ambling by.

"Bob, there you are!" Lani said. "I thought you were going to join us at the Super Nova Infinity Drop. It was transdimensional!"

"Sorry. Got carried away."

"On a baby ride?" she said.

I pointed to the sign. "Technically, you have to be at least three."

"Well, glad you liked it, Bob. But dinner and birthday cake are in half an hour. Promise you won't miss that, right?"

I patted my stomach. "Are you kidding? I wouldn't miss dinner for anything!"

Lani smiled. "Great. Wear your best suit. And see you then!"

★ ★ ★ ★ ★

SPLOG ENTRY #6:
Not Suited for This

Since it took less than a minute to change, and only twenty-five to nap off the excitement of the balloon ride, I was a whole minute early to dinner. (See, I could be on time after all!)

A man in a tuxedo gave me a funny look, then opened the door to the ballroom. "This way, sir."

I leaned toward Beep. "I'm kind of getting to like all this sir stuff."

"Ooh," Beep said, blinking at sparkling chandeliers that dangled over round, white clothed tables as far as the eye could see.

I saw Lani sitting down and headed to her table. "Well, we made it," I announced.

Lani looked at me and froze. "Bob, are you wearing a bathing suit?!"

"My best one." I gulped. "Isn't that what you said?"

"I meant best *formal* suit. This is a luxury star cruiser. Did you really think we were eating poolside?!"

Beep hid his towel behind his back.

Lani heard her name being called and hissed, "My parents are coming! Please, Bob, try to make a good impression."

Beep reached into his pouch and pulled out a red button.

"Where'd you get that?" I said.

He jabbed it frantically. "Yank off wall."

"Beep, it's not going to work now that it's—" Before I could finish, our friendly steward appeared by our side.

"Does the young gentleman require a jacket?" he asked, slipping one over my shoulders.

"Uh, thanks," I said, stepping behind a chair so Lani's parents wouldn't notice my bare legs. And just in time.

"Mom, Dad," Lani said, "you remember all my friends."

"Of course," her mom said, nodding to the circle of us around the big table. "Good evening, Beep and Bob and Zenith and Flash and Andromeda and the rest. Don't you all look delightful. Please, take your seats."

"Thank you," we all said, except for Flash, whose tie was so tight it looked like he might pass out. I kind of hoped he did, so I could steal his pants. Lani sat on one side of me and Beep on the other.

A waiter wearing a hat was walking by our table. I waved to him. "Excuse me, can we get a couple cheeseburgers here?"

Lani's mother gasped. "Young man, that is no way to address the ship's captain!"

"C-captain?" I stammered.

He turned my way, and I braced myself for a stern lecture. But instead he bowed and said, "Captain Smith, at your service."

"Oh, in that case," I said, "do you also have fries?"

The captain stroked his beard and laughed. "You have a bold sense of humor, son."

Beep clapped. "Beep want fries too!"

"He likes orange ketchup," I added. "But only if you have it."

"We have everything you can imagine on the *Starship Titanic*," the captain said with a smile. But his face then darkened. "Except escape pods, of course. Those were deemed unnecessary for the One Hundred Percent Safest Ship in the Galaxy."

Flash blanched. "No escape pods! But what if we hit something?"

Captain Smith shrugged. "Eh."

Lani's father stood. "Thank you for gracing us with your presence," he said to the captain. "But I'm sure you have more important tasks to attend to."

"Not really," the captain said. "Computers pretty much run this thing. I spend most of my day on the Super Nova Infinity Drop." He sighed. "Even the ride operators get to push more buttons than I do."

An attendant tugged on the captain's sleeve. "Sir, we are approaching Neptune. You are needed right away."

The captain brightened. "To pilot the ship?"

"To dine with the Neptunian Countess. She just arrived."

The captain hung his head. "Oh." He then made his way to a big table in the center of the room.

"Ooh, look," Zenith said, "here comes the countess now. Isn't she elegant?"

"She's blue," I pointed out.

Beep, who's also blue, clapped.

"What's that sparkly, purple heart-shaped thing on her chest?" I asked.

"That sparkly *thing*," Lani said, "is the most valuable jewel in the solar system: the Heart of Neptune!"

"Yum!" Beep said.

"Not for eating!" I said.

Lani smiled. "Isn't it simply exquisite?"

Then it hit me: I still hadn't found Lani a gift! What was I supposed to do now? I began to push myself away from the table. "Uh, I think I have to go. . . ."

"Dinner is served!" a steward announced, and at once waiters appeared carrying trays.

"Your meal, sir," one said, putting a plate in front of me. "Does the gentleman require anything else?"

Just a perfect, thoughtful birthday present for a super rich girl who probably already owns her own moon. I slumped in my seat. "No, I'm fine."

"Excellent," he said.

But really, I was doomed.

★★★★★

SPLOG ENTRY #7:
This Spells T-R-O-U-B-L-E

After a hearty dinner Lani turned to me and said, "Isn't this exciting? Soon we'll be orbiting Neptune."

"But we go to school by Saturn," I pointed out. "And Saturn has all those pretty rings."

"Neptune has rings too," she said. "I mean, they may not be as big or well known as Saturn's, but they're still very interesting. The first of the five major rings is made primarily of large ice chunks—"

I braced myself for one of her long science lectures. Luckily, her mother interrupted: "Laniakea, it's almost time for cake. And you're not going to want to miss your *special* surprise."

"Yes, Mom." She leaned toward Beep and me and added, "Don't laugh, but she always has my cake served by costumed TV characters I *used* to think were cool when I was little. It's so embarrassing."

"As long as it's not a clown," I joked, "I'm fine."

Lani smiled.

"Or a magician," I added. "Or a purple dinosaur. Or a—"

"Okay, Bob, we get it."

Out of the corner of my eye, I could see a couple stewards begin to wheel in a table stacked high with wrapped gifts. Ugh. Then the lights suddenly dimmed.

PARTY CRASHERS

"Hey, look," Flash said, pointing across the room. "Is that who I think it is?"

All attention went toward a pair of robots: one tall and golden, the other short and round. The large one carried a cake with flickering candles.

"Oh no," I said.

"My rusty circuits may be mistaken," the larger robot said as he headed our way, "but I do believe we have a birthday girl in the audience."

The little robot spelled, "B-I-R-T-H-D-A-Y. Birthday!"

Beep gasped. "That be . . . that be . . . that be . . . *ABCD-2*! From *Star Words*!" He began to bounce, but I held him down.

In the dim lighting the little alpha-bot kept bumping into people at their seats as he rolled by. Including the Countess!

"Oh dear. I do apologize for his clumsiness," the tall robot, C-345, said.

Lani's mother beamed. "Laniakea, it looks like your favorite *stars* are here."

Lani, reddening, whispered to me, "Yeah, from when I was three."

I struggled to keep Beep from leaping out of his seat. "Well, at least *some*one's excited."

Beep clapped. "ABCD-2! ABCD-2!" Then he jumped from his chair right onto the poor robot, sending him to the floor with a crash.

As I tried to pry Beep off, a panel opened near the top of the ABCD-2 costume. "Hey, buddy," the guy inside said, "you're ruining our gig. Help me up, will you?"

"Sorry about that," I said, struggling with Beep to lift ABCD-2. For a guy in a small costume, he was surprisingly heavy.

C-345 put the cake in front of Lani and said, "Birthdays are F-U-N, fun, children, because we can practice our numbers. How many candles can we count? I see one. I see two. I see three. . . ."

Before he could finish, Lani leaned forward and

blew. The candles went out and everyone clapped.

"Time to spell the birthday song!" C-345 said, and began to sing one letter at a time: "H-A-P-P-Y B-I-R-T-H-D-A-Y T-O Y-O-U! H-A-P-P-Y B-I-R-T-H-D-A-Y T-O . . ."

When he was finally (finally) done, a small cake carving knife came out of ABCD-2 (I could see the guy's hand—it wasn't the most convincing costume ever).

"And with that," C-345 said as the lights came back on, "my little counterpart and I must now say our good-byes. That's G-O-O-D-B-Y-E, good-bye."

When he realized what was happening, Beep leaped forward and clutched ABCD-2 in a tight embrace. "No go! No go!"

A shriek split the room before the robot could reply. Everyone froze.

"My diamond bracelet!" someone screamed. "It's gone!"

"My heirloom watch!" someone cried. "It's gone too!"

Everyone began to look down. Lani's mother gasped. "My wedding ring!"

"My earrings!"

"My pants!" (That one was me.)

But the greatest cry came from the center of the room, where the Countess of Neptune was frantically clutching at her chest . . . for the priceless Heart of Neptune that was no longer there!

★ ★ ★ ★ ★

SPLOG ENTRY #8:
Exposed!

Within seconds a band of burly security guards burst onto the scene. The doors closed and locked as someone shouted, "NO ONE IS TO LEAVE THIS ROOM!"

Beep held tightly on to ABCD-2. "Bad happen! Beep scared! Want cake!"

I tried to pry him off. "You can't have cake until you let go of this robot. You're crushing the poor guy inside."

"Guy inside?!" Beep unclenched, and the robot rolled quickly away.

"Everyone, freeze!" A woman in a sleek black uniform stepped forward. She tapped her badge. "I am Chief Trappz, head of ship security. I will be in charge of this investigation. If you have any questions, too bad, because I'll be the one asking questions. Isn't this awesome?"

Beep clapped, and the chief shot him a look. Then she came closer. "First question," she said, pointing toward our table. "What flavor is that frosting?"

Lani raised her hand. "Excuse me, but what does frosting have to do with finding the Heart of Neptune?"

Chief Trappz narrowed her eyes. "Did it occur to you, miss, that in the thief's panic at being discovered, they dropped the jewel into the cake, with the intent of later claiming the piece with the indented frosting for themselves, thereby committing the perfect crime?"

"Really?" Lani said.

The chief scooped some frosting up with her finger. "Nah, probably not. I just like frosting." She popped it in her mouth, then summoned her guards with a snap. "We'll start our interrogation here. Check them all."

Lani's mother stood in protest. "But they're just children!"

"Exactly," the chief said. "The least suspicious is always *most* guilty."

"Really?"

Chief Trappz shrugged. "I watch a lot of movies." She then noticed the gift table. "What's inside those boxes, miss?"

"I don't know," Lani said. "Could be anything."

The chief raised her finger. "Exactly! Squad, start there."

Before Lani could stop them, the guards began to rip open her presents. One held up a long tube.

Zenith smiled. "That's from me. It's a time-o-scope. For looking back in time!"

"Keep searching!" the chief barked.

"Uh, actually," I said, "that thing might be good for finding the crook. All you have to do is look back about ten minutes in time and—"

The chief held up her hand. "Excuse me, but this is *my* investigation. And I don't use toys, I use my *wits*. Next gift box, please."

Another guard held up a small device with an arrow.

"Ooh, that's from me," Andromeda said.

Lani smiled. "A Matter Detector. You can program in any substance and it will point to it. I've always wanted one! Thanks."

Andromeda reddened. "I know you like boring science things."

"Uh, forgive me for pointing this out," I said to Chief Trappz, "but I bet if you programmed that matter finder thing for *jewels*, it would—"

"Enough!" she said. "Next."

As Lani watched, the guards opened everything. And big surprise, no Heart of Neptune anywhere.

The chief sighed. "I suppose I have to move on to the next table." Finally!

Lani raised her hand. "Excuse me, but are you sure those were *all* of the gifts?"

"It's probably best not to bother the chief," I whispered.

"But, Bob," Lani said. "I haven't seen *your* gift yet. You're a good friend, so I know it must be special."

I felt every eye in the room upon me.

"Well?" Zenith said. "Do you have a gift for her or not?"

"Of course he has something," Lani said. "Bob is always so thoughtful."

"Then, where is it?"

I could feel my heart pounding. How was I going to get out of this one? It was too late to buy her anything. I didn't even know how to fold cool napkin animals. No, even though it would be hard, there was probably only one sure solution: the truth.

"I . . . I got you something super special," I said, "but then a black hole formed and my gift fell inside, and so I went back to the gift shop but some aliens attacked and stole all my money, and so all I had left was some gum to give you, but then . . . then . . . then . . ."

The look in her eyes told me I was doomed. There was only one thing left to do. I spun and pointed. "Beep didn't get you anything either!"

The crowd gasped. "Beep, is that true?" Lani asked.

Beep jumped. "No true! No true!" He pulled half a pencil out of his pouch and smiled.

"That's your present?"

"And *this*!" Beep said, pulling out the other half. But when Lani didn't smile, Beep said, "Wait, must be even more." He fished around in his pouch. "Hmm, what this?"

"Seriously, Beep," Lani said, "you don't have to—"

"Ta-da!" Beep said, pulling out a new find. "Beep get special shiny just for you!"

But Lani, along with everyone else, only gasped at the enormous purple jewel in Beep's hand.

The Heart of Neptune!

★★★★★

SPLOG ENTRY #9:
An Arresting Development

could hardly believe what I was seeing. Beep, the sweetest little alien ever, would never steal. It was impossible!

Then again, that valuable heart-shaped rock *was* in his hand.

Chief Trappz folded her arms. "I rest my case. Guards, arrest the guilty party."

Beep clapped. "Party, yay! Now cake?" But his

happiness turned to confusion when the guards bound his arms behind him.

"Wait!" I said. "Beep is innocent! He was never properly taught right from wrong."

The chief huffed. "So you're saying we should arrest his *parents*?"

I nodded. "Exactly."

"Fine. Where are they?"

"Well, that's hard to say, because—"

Beep pointed at me. "Bob-mother Beep mother! Bob-mother Beep mother!"

The chief rolled her eyes. "Cuff him, too."

As they led us away, I tried to catch Lani's eyes. But the second I did, she glanced down.

"Lani-friend no like shiny?" Beep said to me.

"Not if it belongs to the Neptunian Countess!"

Beep hung his head. "Beep only try make happy."

"I know you did," I said. "But people aren't happy with gifts you *steal*."

"Beep no steal!" he said. "Beep find."

"Yeah. In your *pouch*. Which doesn't exactly look very good. The main question is, how did it get there?"

Beep shrugged. "Fall from space?"

"Not very likely," I said.

"Beep eat by mistake?"

"Possible, I guess."

"Bob-mother put there?"

"Not me!" I said. "But I think you may be on the right track. Like Chief Trappz said, the real thief must have panicked when they learned we were all about to be searched. So they got near enough to plant it on you. But who?"

And then it hit me. I turned to the guards. "Wait!

Stop! I know who stole the Heart of Neptune! And all the other stuff too."

"Tell it to the judge," a guard replied as he halted us in front of an open door.

"Is this"—I gulped—"the ship's jail?"

The guard leaned closer and grinned. "Worse. These are your *quarters*."

I looked inside. "Hey, Beep, he's right. This is our room! Well, that's not so bad. We still have over twelve million channels and—"

"Your quarters," the guard went on, "with all the electronics turned *off*!"

"Wait, what? You mean no TV? No video games? No Internet? No—"

"No nothing!" he said. He uncuffed us and shoved us inside.

★ ★ ★ ★ ★

SPLOG ENTRY #10:
That Sinking Feeling

WARNING: The next entry is going to be very grim. Please skip ahead if you are sensitive to terrible situations—in this case a boy and his friend being deprived of the most basic of kids' rights: lots of glowing screens!

"Beep, this is bad," I said after what felt like ages. "Without something to watch, I'm starting to actually hear my own thoughts. I don't know how much more I can take. How long have we been in here?"

Beep pulled his watch out of his pouch. "Minute."

"There's nothing to do! I'm lost in a fog. I have to get out of here!"

"Now *two* minute."

I took a deep breath. "There must be some kind of entertainment here. Think, Beep, think."

He pointed to the large picture window. Outside, the spectacular view of Neptune filled the frame. "Planet pretty!"

"Maybe if I just pretend it's a movie," I said. I sat

on the floor. "See, it's almost like a giant screen." But within seconds I could feel myself fidget. "Beep, nothing's happening. It's just a big, beautiful, scenic wonder!"

He pointed. "Ooh, Neptune do have rings. Tasty blue!"

I squinted at the thin bands encircling the planet. They grew larger as we approached, but that was about it.

"Sorry, Beep, but I think I'm going to die from boredom now. It was nice knowing you."

"Nice know Bob-mother, too. Beep have Bob-mother gum when gone?"

I clutched my backpack. "No, you cannot have my gum!"

"When Beep have cake?"

I gently put my hand on his shoulder. "Beep, I

don't know how to break this to you—but I don't think they're going to give us any."

His eyes began to well with tears. "Beep sad!"

"Oh, don't cry, Beep. Here, you can have my gum. Take it all."

He reached into my backpack. "This gum big. But Beep eat anyway."

"Wait, Beep, that's not gum." I grabbed it away. "This is a *book*. For my history assignment on that big famous ship that sailed across the ocean." I opened it eagerly. "Can you see how desperate I am, Beep? I'm actually excited to *read*. Now, where was I?"

I flipped to the middle. Luckily, there were lots of pictures. "Here's where I left off: 'The great steamship *Titanic* was only days into its voyage when the unthinkable happened: It hit an iceberg and began to sink.' Wait, what?"

I flipped ahead, narrating the key moments: "Unsinkable ship takes on more water; then more water; then *more* water; and soon it sinks completely into the sea. Beep, this is horrible!"

Beep's eyes welled again. "Story end sad!"

I slammed it shut. "Who knew that history had a *bad* side? Luckily, nothing like that can ever happen again, though, right?"

"But this ship name *Titanic* too," Beep said.

"Yeah, but this one is one hundred percent *safe*."

"Other *Titanic* safe too."

"Yeah, but that one hit an *ice*berg." I folded my arms. "And lucky for us, Beep, there are no icebergs in space."

Beep turned to the window. "No, but ice *ring*."

I spun. "Huh?"

Beep clapped. "Pretty blue ring *big* now!"

The rings of Neptune were big . . . and getting bigger. I realized that we were on a collision course headed straight for them! And with the captain and everyone else in the ballroom, we were the only ones who knew.

So, with certain disaster imminent, I did what I do best:

"GAAAAAAAAAAAAAAAAAAAAAAAA AAAAHHH!"

★ ★ ★ ★ ★

SPLOG ENTRY #11:
Five Icy Rings

WARNING: If you skipped the last splog entry because of how grim I said it was going to be, you may want to skip back, because things are about to get *much* worse. Or maybe skip back two entries. That would be even safer.

On the other hand, two splogs ago is when Beep got caught with the jewel. And that's what started this whole mess! So you may want to skip back even farther. Maybe to the balloon ride part. The Balloon Blast is a ride for four-year-olds, but it's pretty much the best thing that's happened to me this entire trip. Pretty sad, huh? Who writes these things?

Oh, wait, *I* do.

"And Beep draw!" Beep said, holding up a pencil half. (Then he ate it.)

I dared to glance out the window. While planetary rings may look all pretty and smooth from a distance, up close they're really just an asteroidlike field of giant flying ice cubes.

"AHHH!" I shrieked as one ice boulder hit the glass.

"Ooooh!" Beep said.

"AHHH!" I shrieked as another one hit.

"Ooooh!"

I banged on the door. "LET US OUT! LET US OUT! WE'RE GETTING *PULVERIZED*!"

A muffled voice of one of the guards answered, "Not likely. You're just trying to trick us into letting you go."

"No, I swear! The ship is heading directly into one of Neptune's rings!"

"Nice try, kid. But you're thinking of *Saturn*."

"Go to a window!" I said. "Neptune has rings too!"

"Yeah, sure it does."

I repeated what Lani had told me earlier: "They

may not be as big or well known as Saturn's, but they're still very interesting. The first of the five major rings is made primarily of large ice chunks—"

"Yawn, kid. We're going for a coffee break."

"NO, WAIT!" But they were gone.

I spun. "Beep, we have to do something! Beep? Where are you?"

Then a mattress passed over my head and I ducked.

"WHEEEEEEEE!" Beep said from the flying bed. So I guess they hadn't turned *everything* off.

"Beep, get down from there!"

He landed the bed. "But fly fun."

"There's a time for fun, Beep, and a time for thinking of ways to get out of life threatening situations. You know what time *this* is, Beep?"

He pulled out his watch. "Twenty o'clock?"

"Time to think of a plan!"

Beep touched his chin and put on his best thinking look, but it was too late.

"Oh no!" I said as the glass was pummeled again and the sound of cracking grew. "THE WINDOW'S ABOUT TO *BLOOOOOOOOW*!"

★★★★★

SPLOG ENTRY #12:
The Good, the Bad, and the Smelly

Good news! When the glass shattered, all the tiny shards didn't shoot in toward me and Beep, like I feared, but whooshed out into space.

Bad news! All the air whooshed out too.

Good news! Just before I got whooshed out with everything else, Beep swooped down on the flying bed and pulled me aboard.

Bad news: The bed then got whooshed out as well.

Good news!: Beep can breathe in space without a space suit.

Bad news: I can't.

Good news!: Now that I knew how my history book ended, I could give my presentation on Monday.

Bad news: I'd never make it to Monday!

Good news!: Just as I was about to pass out, Beep did something super smart, and shoved my entire head into his pouch, which still had air in it.

Bad news: His pouch smells like socks.

Good news!: Beep was a total expert at flying the bed and zipped it all the way to one of the ship's air lock doors.

Bad news: My head was still in his pouch.

Good news!: Beep got us back inside the ship again, where I could breathe.

Bad news: Everything *still* smelled like socks.

I hacked. "Beep, thanks for saving my life and all," I said, "but have you ever considered washing that thing out?"

Beep pouted. "Beep no like bath."

"Well, you're lucky, then, Beep, because there's no time for a bath. We have to get back to the ballroom. Now!"

We ran through the halls, burst through the doors, and raced to our table. "Lani!" I said. "It's okay, Beep and I are alive. But you should have seen what we went through."

"I did," she said.

"What do you mean?"

She held up her phone. "One of the passengers on the upper deck caught you on video. See?" She showed me footage of Beep flying the bed out in space, with my head stuck in his pouch. "It's only been posted on the intergalactic Internet for ten minutes, yet it's already a big hit!"

The number of hysterical laughing face emojis below the video was up to five trillion.

"Oh, great," I said.

Lani hushed me. "Shhh. The captain's making an announcement."

"Good news!" the captain said. "The *Starship Titanic* has now cleared the rings of Neptune. We will not sustain any more damage."

People cheered.

"Bad news," he continued. "Many windows were broken, as well as some large screen TVs."

The crowd murmured.

"Good news!" he went on. "Those are all easily repairable."

People cheered.

"Bad news," he said. "The main thrusters have also been damaged, and thus the ship is unable to fly."

The crowd murmured.

"Good news!" the captain said. "The band is ready to play for this evening's entertainment."

People clapped.

"Bad news," he said. "Without the thrusters, the

ship will plummet hopelessly toward the giant planet below, and since there are no escape pods on board, tonight's entertainment will be the last you ever hear. Please enjoy!"

★ ★ ★ ★ ★

SPLOG ENTRY #13:
Beep Blow Big Blue Bubble

Within moments the room erupted in panic. People screamed and ran. I could barely even hear the music.

Beep sat calmly at the table.

"Beep, why aren't you freaking out like everyone else?!" I asked.

"Beep wait for cake."

I eyed all the crumb filled plates. "Looks like they already ate it all."

Beep's eyes widened. "Cake gone?"

"Cake gone."

"NOOOOOOOOOOOO!" he cried, joining the rest of the pandemonium.

"Here," I said to distract him. "Have some gum."

"Pepperminty, yum!" Beep said.

I popped the last piece in my own mouth, mainly to try to get rid of the sock smell.

Across from us, Lani's father grabbed the captain. "There must be some way you can save us!"

"Lift this enormous ship from the gravitational pull of a planet?" the captain said. "I'm a pilot, not a miracle worker. And not even much of a pilot anymore."

"Then we demand a refund."

The captain pointed. "The refund line's over there."

I turned to Beep. "This is hopeless. What are we going to do?"

Beep blew a blue bubble with his gum and clapped. But his clap popped the bubble, so he had to start again.

"Beep, you're forgetting what I told you about life threatening situation time."

He pouted.

"Now, think hard, Beep, because we—wait, that's it. You're a genius!"

"Beep genius?"

I grabbed his arm. "Quick, this way!"

We passed Lani, who said, "Where are you going, Bob?"

I lifted a finger high. "To the amusement park!"

"Really, Bob? Really?"

"It's not what you think—"

"No, go ahead," she said. "Have your fun."

I kept running. "No time to explain!"

We passed a window, and I tried not to peek at the looming planet below. If my plan didn't work, it wouldn't be long until we went zooming smack into its atmosphere.

I panted as we ran. The bummer about gravity was it made you have to exercise. "Up these stairs, Beep. I think"—*pant*—"we're almost there."

And then, suddenly, there it was: the gate to the amusement parks! Luckily, no one was there. We ran inside. Right up to the . . .

"Balloon Blast!" Beep said. He sat on a chair.

I pulled him off. "Not yet. First, we have to lift the Balloon-o-Matic. And get it to the—I forget what you call the front of a ship. Oh, wait, now I remember: bow."

Beep bowed.

"No, that's the official name for the front of a ship: bow."

Beep bowed again.

"Just help me pick it up!"

We struggled to lift the machine. That was another problem with gravity: It made things heavy. Just as we were getting a good grip on the machine though, a voice boomed from behind.

"STOP RIGHT THERE!"

I spun to see Chief Trappz and her guards.

"Oh, am I glad to see you," I said. "We could really use some help lifting this to the bow."

Beep bowed, dropping his side of the machine.

The chief put her hands on her waist. "Caught you thieves red-handed this time."

"What? No," I said. "We're not thieves!"

"You're stealing that balloon-making thing right before my eyes!"

"Yes, but for a very good reason!" I argued.

She pulled out two pairs of handcuffs.

"Tell it to the judge."

The rest of the guards surrounded us. It was no use resisting. I held up my hands. "I guess we have to know when to quit, Beep." I turned. "Beep?"

Before I knew what was happening, Beep grabbed me tight and we, along with the Balloon-o-Matic, were lifted up into the air. Using his alien wits, Beep had programmed the Balloon-o-Matic to make hundreds of balloons to carry us away!

The guards shouted and jumped to catch us and the Balloon-o-Matic. But we were too high.

"Beep!" I said. "You really are a genius."

Beep bowed.

"Now, get us to the bo—front of the ship, Beep. And get ready to make *history*!"

★★★★★

SPLOG ENTRY #14:
Captain Courageous

Good news! We lost the guards and found a small air lock door at the bow of the ship!

Bad news: Beep suddenly needed a bathroom break.

Good news!: After his break, Beep went through the air lock so he could tie a billion balloons to the railing!

Bad news: He forgot to take the Balloon-o-Matic out with him.

Good news!: He came back inside to get it!

Bad news: He remembered he forgot to wash his hands and went back to the bathroom.

Good news!: Beep came back from the bathroom, took the Balloon-o-Matic out through the air lock, set it for a billion balloons, pushed the button, and finally saved the day!

When he was back inside for good, I brushed my hands together. "Well, I'd say we *tied* that problem into a pretty neat knot, huh, Beep? Get it? *Tied!*"

Beep clapped. "Yay tied!" Then he shrugged. "What mean 'tied'?"

"Tied. Like with a string. Like how you *tied* the balloons to the ship." I froze. "You did *tie* the balloons to the ship, didn't you?"

Beep pinched his chin. "Hmmm . . ."

I glanced out the hatch, at the balloons' strings that were floating up . . . up . . . up.

"GET BACK OUT THERE, BEEP! HURRY!"

"But Beep forgot wash hands again."

"Why would you need to wash your hands again?!"

"Beep touch balloon. And kids touch balloon too. Yech."

"They didn't touch *those* balloons."

Beep clapped. "That good. Beep go tie now!"

Luckily, he caught them just in time. And *tied* them until they held. The strings tightened, and the *Starship Titanic* began to lift away from the planet. (Note: Even though balloons don't technically work in space, because space doesn't have an atmosphere, these were special *space gas* balloons. Just go with it.)

When Beep was safely back inside, I collapsed. "Whew, that was close. But we're big heroes now, Beep!"

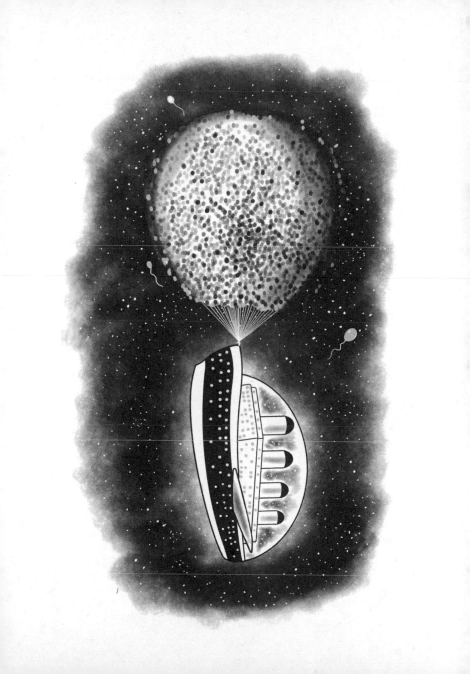

Beep clapped. "Hero!"

I turned at the sound of voices. "Look, here comes Lani, the captain, and the whole gang now. Probably to give us some medals and stuff."

"Bob," Lani said, running up, "what have you done?!"

I folded my arms. "Saved the day, I'd say."

She pointed. "And I'd say we're about to collide with those rings again! Untie the balloons or we'll all die!"

She was right. The ship was headed right toward the icy rings!

"But without the balloons," I said, "we'll crash into the planet!"

"But with the balloons," she argued, "we'll crash into the rings!"

"But without the balloons," I countered, "we'll crash into the planet!"

"But with the balloons—"

Luckily, Captain Smith interrupted: "Stop, both of you! There's only one way to survive. And that's if someone expertly steers the ship through the narrow rings until we are free!" He glanced around. "By any chance, can anyone here do that?"

"Uh, *you're* the captain," I said.

"Yes," he said, "but the computer does all the *actual* navigating. And when it saw what danger we were in, it turned itself off!"

"Can't you call tech support?" I said. "I'm sure this ship has it!"

He held up his phone. "I did, but I'm on hold!"

My panic was renewed. "We're never going to make it!"

"Wait!" Lani said to the captain. "Surely you must have piloted a ship back when you weren't so ancient?"

He stroked his white beard. "When I was a wee

lad, I played with holo-ships in the virtual bath. But those were simpler times."

Beep shuddered. "Beep hate bath!"

"Please, Captain Smith," Lani said. "You at least have to try!"

The captain looked ahead, and a fire began to burn in his eyes. "You're right. I am the captain. I can do this!" He spun. "To the wheelhouse I go!"

The rings loomed ever closer as we waited for the captain to get to the wheelhouse.

"Brace yourself, Beep!" I said.

The rings came closer. And closer. And so close the uppermost balloons began to pop!

"We're not going to make it!" I said.

"No, look, we're veering left!" Lani pointed out.

"Then right!" I said.

Lani stumbled. "Then left again!"

I grabbed hold of a chair. "Then a little jog to the right!"

"Beep too tired for jog," he said.

"Then left and . . . we made it!"

Everyone cheered.

"Thank you, thank you," the captain said as he came back down. He dabbed his eyes. "Guess I am a real captain after all."

Lani smiled. "Guess that's that."

I wiped my brow. "Finally. I mean, this was like one of those horrible movies where you think it's over about twenty times, but there's always one last—"

"EVERYONE RUN!" someone shouted. "WE'RE ABOUT TO CRASH INTO TRITON, THE LARGEST OF NEPTUNE'S FOURTEEN MOONS!"

"Uh, be right back," Captain Smith said.

And then, with one more *big* swerve to the left, that truly was that.

★ ★ ★ ★ ★

SPLOG ENTRY #15:
And the Band Finally Stopped

The birthday party group and many other guests gathered back in the ballroom to celebrate. The band was still playing.

"How noble," the captain said to the musicians at the end of their song. "You played on even as the ship plummeted to certain doom."

The musicians looked up in confusion.

"Wait!"

"Huh?"

"What?"

The captain then came to our table. "I just want to thank you all for encouraging me," he said. "After what the other Captain Smith, my ancestor from long ago, did to the original *Titanic*, I have now cleared my family name."

I pulled out my history book. "Hey, I know about that! But if you knew about it too, then why did you give this ship the same name?"

He shrugged. "Probably not the best idea."

"I don't suppose," I said, "that you can come to my class on Monday and help me with my history report?"

The captain beamed. "I'd be honored, son. I can talk for *hours* about the *Titanic*!"

"Uh, hours?" I said.

He put his arms around me and Beep. "It's the least I can do for two heroes."

The Neptunian Countess stood. "JUST ONE MOMENT," she said, pointing to us. "Aren't you forgetting that those two are *thieves*?!"

Oh, yeah, that. "No, wait!" I said. "Beep and I are innocent. But I know who the real thieves are. And they're right here in this room!"

Everyone gasped. Chief Trappz and her guards burst into the room.

"Don't worry, they won't escape now!" the chief said, blocking the doors.

"Thief where?!" Beep said. "Thief where?!"

I sighed. "Sorry, Beep, but you're not going to like this. The ones who stole the Heart of Neptune and all the other stuff, and then tried to frame you, are right"—I spun and pointed toward the stage—"there!"

The musicians froze.

"Wait!"

"Huh?"

"What?"

"No, not you!" I said to the musicians. "*Next* to the stage. Quick, they're getting away!"

"Get them!" Chief Trappz commanded.

Within seconds, they were surrounded.

Beep ran to ABCD-2. "Say no so! Say no so!"

A panel on the small robot slid open. And a metal utensil popped out!

"Look out, Beep!" I cried. "He has an ice cream scoop!"

Another panel on the costume slid open, revealing a face. "It was a perfect plan!" he said. "In this costume I could *bump* into anyone, and then snatch and hide the jewels inside! But when I saw they were looking for the big heart-shaped one, I knew I had to dump it. And what better place than the pouch of the little alien who was giving me a hug? We would have gotten away with it too, if it weren't for you meddling kids!"

C-345 kicked the small robot. "Way to admit our crimes, Frank."

ABCD-2 held the scoop higher. "There's still time to escape! And no one can stop us!"

"Oh yeah?" Beep said, and began to jab his red button.

The steward appeared. "You called, sir?"

Beep pointed at the robots. "They need jacket!"

"Of course," the steward said. "One for you"—he draped C-345's head in a tuxedo—"and one for you," he added, smothering ABCD-2 and knocking him to the floor.

ABCD-2's top popped off, and the rest of the

stolen jewels spilled out. The guards pounced in for the arrest.

The steward turned to Beep. "And the new cake you ordered will be out momentarily, sir."

Beep opened his arms. "Happy hug!"

"Of course, sir."

The captain folded his arms. "The stewards here really are top-notch."

"Only the best for my daughter on her birthday," Lani's mother said.

"Birthday!" I said, suddenly remembering. I turned to Lani and hung my head. "Lani, I'm really sorry that I never got you a birthday present. And then sorry I lied about it. And then sorry—"

"Bob, it's okay," Lani said with a smile. "You and Beep caught the crooks and kind of helped save the ship. And most of all, you came to my party. And that's the best gift a girl can have. Well, short of an interdimensional pony."

"Happy hug!" Beep said again, this time to Lani.

The steward lifted Beep into Lani's embrace.

Luckily, I'm not the type who needs that kind of affection. Lani's thanks were reward enough, and, like the captain, I was content to stand tall and—

To my surprise, the steward then lifted me up and plopped me into Lani's open arms too.

And Bob thought, "Yay."

★★★★★

SPLOG ENTRY #16:
A Night to Remember

After Beep ate most of the giant new cake, and Lani's parents and the captain began to drink coffee and gab, Lani suggested we go off for one last fun activity before bedtime.

Beep clapped. "Balloon Blast, Balloon Blast!"

"We stole that one, Beep," I said. "Remember?"

Beep pouted. "Now Beep do."

"Don't worry," Lani said, "I know something even better!"

I crossed my fingers and thought, *Super Nova Infinity Drop, Super Nova Infinity Drop, Super Nova Infinity Drop.* After all I'd been through today, I finally felt brave enough to try it.

I shrugged. "You mean, like the, uh—what's that one called? Oh, yeah, the Super Nova Infinity Something?"

"Drop," Lani said. "Actually, I was thinking more of a stroll along the top deck. Under the stars."

"Uh—stroll?" I said, wondering if I had heard her right. "Under *stars*?"

She lifted her foot. "It feels good to actually walk for a change, instead of float, don't you think?"

Beep shook his head. "Beep like flying bed!"

I had to admit, after hours of all this gravity, I was getting a little tired of using my legs again too.

Lani smiled. "You can't say no to a birthday girl, now, can you?"

"Uh, no," I said. "I mean yes. I mean . . ."

Lani took off, and since there really was no arguing, Beep and I followed.

And you know what?

We walked along the deck, and we talked about silly things, and we peered up at the stars as they flickered down upon the great *Starship Titanic*. And it was totally nice and boring.

Just like I like it.

SEND

★ ★ ★ ★ ★

Bob's Extra-Credit Fun Space Facts! (Even though nothing is fun about space!)

Neptune is the eighth planet from the sun. It was discovered by astronomers in 1846, but they didn't find it with telescopes—they found it using **math**! (Guess math has some uses after all. Who knew?)

More than a hundred years later they also discovered that Neptune has five major **rings** around it, made of floating ice chunks the size of Texas,

THOUGH NO ONE EVER BELIEVES THIS UNTIL YOU'RE ABOUT TO RUN INTO THE RINGS, AND EVEN THEN THEY STILL THINK YOU'RE TALKING ABOUT **SATURN**! Neptune is also a pretty shade of blue.

Neptune was named after the **Roman** god of the sea, whose name was **Neptune**. Neptune was also the god of horses, but that doesn't make much sense, because horses live on land. Speaking of horses, once at this fair my little sister and I went on a pony ride. My sister was mad because I got a pony with a unicorn horn and she didn't. I knew it was a pretend horn, but I still thought it was pretty cool.

Anyway, that's what I know about Neptune.

★ ★ ★ ★ ★

ACKNOWLEDGMENTS

The author would like to thank NASA for use of their photographs as source material.

READ THE NEXT BEEP AND BOB ADVENTURE:

TAKE US TO YOUR SUGAR

★ ★ ★ ★ ★

SPLOG ENTRY #1
Send Snacks!

Dear Kids of the Past,

Hi. My name's Bob and I live and go to school in space. That's right, space. Pretty sporky, huh? Only a hundred Earth kids are picked to go to Astro Elementary each year, and I was one of them. There's just one micro little problem:

THE FOOD!

I mean, they have the technology to make anything,

but the only pizza toppings in our cafeteria are broccoli bits and proton sprinkles!

Beep just said, "Sprinkles, yum!" Beep is a young alien who got separated from his 600 siblings when they were playing hide-and-seek in some asteroid field. Then he floated around space for awhile, until he ended up here. Sad, huh?

You know what's even sadder? I was the one who found him knocking on our space station's air lock door and let him in. Now he thinks I'm his new mother! Obviously Beep can be very confused (especially about food, since he *tastes* with his eyes).

But I still like him.

"Beep like Bob-mother, too!"

Beep is pretty good at drawing, so I let him do all the pictures for these space logs (splogs, as we call them). Unfortunately his pencils are yellow, so he thinks they taste like banana. It's not even snack time, and he's already gone through a dozen!

Anyway, that's my life. Enjoy!